The Adventures of a Bear, and a Great Bear too

by Alfred Elwes

Copyright © 3/16/2016
Jefferson Publication

ISBN-13: 978-1530596041

Printed in the United States of America

Table of Contents

AT HOME.

Yes, it is an "at home" to which I am going to introduce you; but not the at-home that many of you—I hope *all* of you—have learnt to love, but the at-home of a bear. No carpeted rooms, no warm curtains, no glowing fireside, no pictures, no sofas, no tables, no chairs; no music, no books; no agreeable, cosy chat; no anything half so pleasant: but soft moss or snow, spreading trees, skies with ever-changing, tinted clouds, some fun, some rough romps, a good deal of growling, and now and then a fight. With these points of difference, you may believe the *at-home* of a bear is not quite so agreeable a matter as the at-home of a young gentleman or lady; yet I have no doubt Master Bruin is much more at his ease in it than he would find himself if he were compelled to conform to the usages of human society, and behave as a gentleman ought to do.

But there is a quality that is quite as necessary to adorn one home as the other, without which the most delightful mansion and the warmest cavern can never be happy, and with which the simplest cottage and the meanest den may be truly blest; and that one quality is, good temper. Of what avail are comforts, or even luxuries, when there is no seasoning of good temper to enjoy them with? How many deficiencies can there not be overlooked, when good temper is present to cover them with a veil? Perhaps you have not yet learnt what a valuable treasure this good temper is; when you have read the history of my bear, you will be better able to form an opinion.

I cannot tell you when this bear was born, nor am I quite sure where; bears are born in so many parts of the world now, that it becomes very difficult to determine what country heard their first growl, and they never think to preserve a memorandum of the circumstance. Let it suffice that our bear was born, that he had a mamma and papa, and some brothers and sisters; that he lived in a cavern surrounded by trees and bushes; that he was always a big lump of a bear, invariably wore a brown coat, and was often out of temper, or rather, was always *in* temper, only that temper was a very bad one.

No doubt his parents would have been very willing to cure this terrible defect, if they had known how; but the fact is, they seemed always too much absorbed in their own thoughts to attend much to their family. Old Mr. Bruin would sit in his corner by the hour together sucking his paw; and his partner, Mrs. Bruin, would sit in her corner sucking her paw; whilst the little ones, or big ones, for they were growing up fast, would make themselves into balls and roll about the ground, or bite one another's ears by way of a joke, or climb up the neighbouring trees to admire the prospect, and then slip down again, to the imminent destruction of their clothes; not that a rent or two would have grieved their mother very much, for she was a great deal too old, and too ignorant besides, to think of mending them. In all these sports Master Bruin, the eldest, was ever the foremost; but as certain as he joined in the romps, so surely were uproar and fighting the consequence. The reason was clear enough; his temper was so disagreeable, that although he was quite ready to play off his jokes on others, he could never bear to receive them in return; and being, besides, very fierce and strong, he came at length to be considered as the most unbearable bear that the forest had known for many generations, and in his own family was looked on as quite a bug-bear.

Now I privately think, that if a good oaken stick had been applied to his shoulders, or any other sensitive part of his body, whenever he displayed these fits of spleen, the exercise would have had a very beneficial effect on his disposition; but his father, on such occasions, only uttered his opinion in so low a growl that it was impossible to make out what he said, and then sucked his paw more vigorously than ever; and his mother was much too tender-hearted to think of mending his manners in so rude a way: so Master Bruin grew apace, until his brothers and sisters were wicked enough to wish he might some day go out for a walk and forget to come home again, or that he might be persuaded by a kind friend to emigrate, without going through the ceremony of taking leave of his family.

It began to be conjectured that some such event had occurred when, for three whole days, he never made his appearance. The respectable family of the Bruins were puzzled, but calm, notwithstanding, at this unusual absence; it evidently made them thoughtful, though it was impossible to guess what they thought about: if one could form an idea from the attitudes of the different members, each of whom sat in a corner sucking his right paw and his left paw alternately—it was a family habit, you must know—I should say their thoughts were too deep for expression; but before their meditations were converted from uncertainty into mourning, the object of them made his appearance at the entrance of the cavern, with his coat torn, limping in his gait, and with an ugly wound in his head, looking altogether as disconsolate a brute as you can well conceive. He did not condescend to say where he had been, nor what he had been doing; perhaps no one made the inquiry: but it was very evident he had been doing no good, and had got his reward accordingly. If, however, this great bear's ill temper was remarkable before, judge what it must have been with such a sore head!

The experience of mankind has led to the opinion, that there are few more disagreeable beings in creation than ill-nurtured bears,—bears that have been ill-licked,—those great, fierce, sullen, cross-grained and ill-tempered beasts, that are, unhappily, to be found in every part of this various world; but when all these unhandsome qualities are found in one individual of the species, and that one happens to have a sore head into the bargain, it is easy to believe the *at home* which he honours or dishonours with his presence can neither be very quiet nor particularly comfortable.

Habit makes many things supportable which at first would seem beyond our powers of endurance. Mr. and Mrs. B., and, indeed, all the other B.'s, male and female, had got so used to the tyranny of this ill-tempered animal, that they put up with his moroseness almost without a growl; but there is a limit to sufferance, beyond which neither men nor bears can travel, and that boundary was at last attained with the B.'s. As what I am now about to relate is, however, rather an important fact in my biography, I must inform you how the matter occurred, and what were the circumstances which led to it.

You are, perhaps, aware that bears, being of rather an indolent disposition, are not accustomed to hoard up a store of provision for their wants in winter, but prefer—in their own country, at least—sleeping through the short dreary days and long bitter nights, and thus avoid the necessity of taking food for some weeks, although they grow very thin during their lengthened slumbers. I forget what this time is called in bears' language, but we give it the name of hybernation. Now it happened that Mrs. Bruin had taken it into her head to lay by this winter a nice little stock, which she very carefully buried at a short distance from the mouth of the cavern, when she felt the usual drowsiness of the season coming on, and having covered the spot with a heap of dead leaves that she might know it again when she woke up, she crawled into bed, and turning her back to her old partner, who was already in a comfortable state of forgetfulness, went fast asleep.

The whole family rather overslept themselves, for the sun was quite brilliant when they awoke, and it was very evident that they had been dozing away for some months. The ill-tempered bear was the first on his legs, and kicking his two nearest brothers as he got up, just to hint to them that he was awake again, he opened his mouth to its whole extent—and a very great extent it was, too—and stretching his limbs one after another, and giving himself a hearty shake instead of washing, shaving, and combing, he scuffled to the entrance of the cavern and sniffed at the fresh air. He sniffed and sniffed, and the more he sniffed, the more certainly did his nose whisper that there was something else besides fresh air which he was inhaling. The smell of the fresh air, too, or the *something else*, caused him a tremendous appetite, which was every moment becoming greater; and then it entered his bearish brain that where there was a smell there must be something to occasion it. Whereupon, following that great nose of his—and he could not have had a better guide—he scuffled out of the cavern and down the path, till he reached a little mound of earth and leaves, where, the odour being strongest, he squatted down. With his great paws he soon demolished the entrance to his mamma's larder, and lost no time in pulling out some of the dainties it contained, which, without more ado, he set about devouring. Meanwhile his brothers, who had been aroused by the affectionate conduct of the eldest, were by this time also wide awake, and had quite as good appetites as Bruin himself; and though on ordinary occasions they stood in great awe of that most ill-tempered brute, it must be admitted that this was an *extra*-ordinary occasion, and they acted accordingly. Just fancy being months without anything to eat, and having appetites fierce enough to devour one another!

So they rushed to the spot where Bruin was making so excellent a meal, and without any other apology than a short grunt or two, they seized upon some of the hidden treasures, and with little ceremony crammed them into their hungry jaws. Bruin was thunderstruck! Never before had they ever presumed to dip their paws into his dish, and now they were actually before his face, converting the most delicate morsels to their own use, and, as it were, taking the food out of his very mouth! After an internal struggle of a few seconds, during which it seemed doubtful whether his emotions or his greediness in filling his jaws so full would choke him, he uttered a savage growl, and, with one stroke of his huge paw, felled his younger brother to the ground. Then turning to the second, he flew at him like a fury, and seemed resolved to make him share a similar fate; but the other, who was not wanting in courage, and who was strengthened by the idea that there was something still in the larder worth fighting for, and which he would certainly lose if he ran away, warded off his blows, and, by careful management, now dodging, now striking, kept his brother at bay, and avoided coming to such close quarters as to subject himself to Bruin's hug: for he knew, if he once felt that embrace, there was not much chance of his having any appetite left with which to complete his half-finished breakfast.

BE

ARS AND BROTHERS.

The noise of the combat had now, however, roused the family. Mrs. B. was the first to make her appearance, and she was soon followed by the rest. Explanations ensued, although the facts of the case were sufficiently clear, and Bruin's character was well known. Old Ursus Major drew himself up, and, for once in his life, assumed a dignified demeanour. The ill-tempered bear stood abashed before his parents, although he moved his head to and fro in an obstinate manner, as though rejecting all interference.

It is a pity I cannot relate to you what was said upon this occasion, for Old Bruin is reported to have made a very eloquent discourse on the horrible effects of ill-temper and greediness; and good advice is worth having, whether uttered by a bear or any other animal. Suffice it, that after lecturing his son on the enormity of his offences,—which probably he was himself partly the cause of, through not punishing many of his previous errors,—he bid him quit for ever his paternal roof, and seek his fortune elsewhere; cautioning him at the same time, that if he ever expected to get through the world with credit to his name, and even comfort to his person, he must be honest, good-tempered, and forbearing.

Bruin took this advice in most ungracious part; and without exchanging a word with any of the family, although it was evident his poor old mother longed to hug him in her arms, he growled out some unintelligible words, and set forth upon his travels.

UPON HIS TRAVELS.

There is no denying that when Bruin had got clear of the old familiar path, and lost sight of the dwelling where he had hitherto spent his days, he felt most particularly uncomfortable; and if he had had the power of recalling the past, he would, in his present state of feeling, no doubt have done so. For the first time in his life, the sense of his ill-temper struck him in all its ugliness; and as he sat down on a huge tree which was lying across his road, he looked such a picture of disconsolateness, that it was evident he would have felt great relief if he could have shed some tears. Alas, how much does Bruin's condition remind us of little scenes among ourselves! We give way to our bad tempers and our selfishness; we make ourselves disagreeable, and our friends unhappy; we quarrel, if we do not actually fight; and when we meet the reward of our waywardness, and find ourselves abandoned by those who would have loved us had we acted differently, we then moan over our fate, and bitterly regret what we might have avoided. Alas, poor human nature! alas, poor bear!

I am truly sorry to observe that no act of repentance followed Bruin's sense of desolation. His first feeling of sorrow over, he felt indignant that he should have been so treated; but, more than that, as he was still hungry, he felt regret at being denied a closer search into his old mother's larder.

Whilst engaged in his various reflections he happened to cast his eyes up to a neighbouring hollow tree, where, at some height from the ground, a number of bees were flying in and out a great hole, with all the bustle and buzzing usual to those busy people. Now, it is well known that bears are mightily fond of honey, and will run great risks in order to obtain this dainty, and Bruin was very far from being an exception to his tribe. He was too ignorant to reflect that it was a great deal too early in the season to hope for any store, but, consulting only his own inclinations, he lost no time in climbing up the tree; and when he had reached the spot where the now angry bees were hurrying to and fro more vigorously than ever, he thrust his great paw into a hole with the hope of drawing forth a famous booty. But the indignant insects now came out in a swarm, and attacked him with the utmost fury; three of them settled on his nose, and pricked him most unmercifully; a dozen or two planted themselves on a great patch behind, where his trousers were worn thin; and a whole troop fastened on to the sore place in his head—for it was not quite healed up—and so stung him, that, roaring with pain and rage, he threw himself, rather than descended, from the tree, and went flying through the wood to get rid of his determined little enemies: they stuck fast, however, to their points of attack, nor did Bruin get clear of his tormentors till he dashed himself into a pool of water and buried his head for a moment or two under the surface.

It was with some degree of trepidation that he raised his nose above water and peeped about him; the bees were all gone, so he crawled out of the mud, and after an angry shake or two, for his coat was quite wet, he resumed his journey.

Bruin now travelled on till noon; and what with hunger and his long walk, you may believe his temper was not improved. A rustling noise on the left, accompanied every now and then with a short, contented kind of grunt, attracted his attention, and looking through some brambles, he descried in an open space a very large boar, with two most formidable tusks protruding from his jaws, busily engaged in rooting up the ground, from which he had extracted a curious variety of roots and other edibles, the sight of which made Bruin's mouth water. For the first time in his life he felt the necessity of civility; for though he had never made any personal acquaintance with the tribe to which the animal before him belonged, there were many tales current in his family of their ferocity when provoked; and the few reasoning powers he possessed were sufficient to assure him, that not even his rough paws or burly strength would secure him from those glistening tusks if directed angrily against him. So Bruin resolved to try and be civil; and with this determination walked into the stranger's domain, and accosted him in as polite a way as his rude nature would permit him to assume.

The animal, who was known in his neighbourhood as Wylde Boare, Esquire, on account of the extent of his property, received Bruin's advances with great caution, for he was naturally of a suspicious temper, his bright reddish eyes twinkling in a very unpleasant manner; perceiving, however, that his unexpected visitor was but a mere youngster, and that he looked very hungry and tired, he grunted out a surly sort of welcome, and, jerking his snout in the direction of the heap of provisions, bade him squat down and make a meal. Bruin did not wait for a second invitation, but, stretching out his huge legs, picked up the fresh vegetables, which he thrust into his capacious jaws with every appearance of relish.

When his repast came to an end—and this did not happen till there was an end of the food—he wiped his mouth with the back of his arm, and looked at the boar; and the boar, who had said nothing during the disappearance of the fruits of his morning's work, but had contented himself with uttering a grunt or two, looked at Bruin. At length he observed,——

"Hurgh, you have a famous appetite!"

"Ah," answered the bear, "and so would you, if you had not eaten anything for the last few weeks!"

After a pause:——

"Hurgh, hurgh!" said Mr. Boare, in a guttural voice; "I never tried; but a big fellow like you ought to be able to get through a deal of work."

"Perhaps so," observed the surly bear; "but I don't intend to make the experiment."

After another pause:——

"Hurgh, an idle fellow, I'm afraid!" said Mr. Boare, half aside; "and not quite so civil as before his breakfast." Then he exclaimed aloud, "I suppose you will make no objection to help me dig up some more food, seeing that you have made away with my dinner, hurgh?"

"Who do you take me for?" said the ungrateful beast, springing to his legs, and eyeing his entertainer with one of his furious looks.

"Who do I take you for, hurgh, you graceless cub?" exclaimed Mr. Boare, in a rage, for he was rather hasty in his manner, and his red eyes twinkled, and his back began to get up in a way which showed his agitation; "who do I take you for? Why, I did take you for one who would be at least thankful for food given you when almost starving: but I now perceive you are only an ugly lump of a bear. Out of my sight this instant, or, from want of my own dinner, which you have devoured, I shall, perchance, make a meal of you!—hurgh, hurgh!"

As he said these words the bristles on his back started up so furiously, and his tusks glistened so horridly in a little ray of sunlight, which was peeping in to see what was the matter, that Master Bruin felt thoroughly frightened, and made a precipitate retreat, turning round at every few steps to observe whether he were followed, and if it would be necessary to take refuge in one of the trees; but Wylde Boare, Esq. only grunted out his favourite expression, which, in this case, was mixed with a great deal of contempt, and recommenced digging for his dinner as if nothing had occurred to disturb his usual contented state of mind.

Bruin now travelled on till he reached a stream, which came bounding through this part of the wood at a very rapid pace, and making a terrible fuss because sundry large stones in the middle of its course rather impeded its progress. The noise it made, and the anger it showed, seemed to please our sulky bear mightily, so he sat down on the bank with his toes in the water to enjoy the spectacle. The scene was a very striking one, and was fitted to charm the most indifferent eye; and Bruin, bear as he was, could not help being attracted by it. Whatever his meditations, however, it was not destined that he should pursue them long without interruption; for his quick ear soon detected the sharp, quick bark of several dogs—a sound that was carried along by a breeze which swept by him at intervals. He raised his head with his huge nose in the air to sniff out any possible danger, and did not seem at all pleased with the result of his observations; for he drew first one foot and then the other out of the water, and raised himself to his full height. As he did so, a more than usual commotion in the stream drew his attention, when he perceived the round head of a large otter appear above the surface, whilst two bright eyes gave a hasty look all round. On observing Bruin, the head immediately disappeared, and at the same moment a whole pack of terriers, in hot haste, came sweeping round a bank hard by, but stopped short on finding themselves in presence of such a formidable creature.

Bruin perceived that he had made an impression, and his usual insolence returned; for he had at first been startled, and he attributed the pause of the terriers to fear, when, in fact, it was only the result of surprise. If he had been a little better physiognomist, he would have observed a certain air of determination about the little fellows, which sufficiently showed that it was prudence or a sense of duty which stayed them, and not a lack of courage: they had been sent out to procure an otter, and they were now deliberating among themselves whether it would be wise to spend their time in quarrelling with a bear.

A CLOSE EMBRACE.

After a short consultation, one who appeared to have the guidance of the pack uttered a decided little bark, and turning a little aside, endeavoured to pass between Bruin and the stream, but sufficiently near to show that he was not afraid to come into contact with him, followed by his companions. This evidently contemptuous mode of treating him, aroused all our ill-tempered hero's bad humour; so, without considering the consequences of the action, he raised his big paw and knocked the leader down. The sturdy little fellows wanted no further provocation; as if influenced by a single will, they turned upon him, and attacked him in front, flank, and rear, with an impetuosity which was at first irresistible, because unexpected. Finding that those behind him were his greatest and most successful tormentors, he very prudently sat himself down, crushing one or two of them in his descent; then springing to his legs, and as he did so catching several more in his arms, he hugged them till they had no more breath in their bodies, when he dropped them, and took up a fresh supply. One of the pack, however, more alert than his fellows, sprang up and seized him by the nose, making his teeth meet in that prominent feature, and caused Bruin such intense pain, that, forgetting all his strategy, he tried to beat down his determined little foe with his paws, and ran off howling in a most terrific manner, pursued by the remainder of the pack, who bit at his hind legs, tore his already ragged coat till it hung in ribbons; and when Bruin, who, having at length got rid of the bold little fellow that had fastened to his nose, climbed up a tree, they stood yelping at the foot of it, till evening had completely set in, when they slowly retired.

And what were our ill-natured hero's thoughts, as he sat upon an elevated branch, and gently rubbed his wounded snout? Why, unfortunately for his own happiness, he laid the blame of his mishap on any one or any thing, rather than the right being or circumstance. It was the otter's fault, or the dogs' fault—those dogs were always so quarrelsome; or it was his father's fault in driving him away from home: in fact, every one was in error rather than himself and his own disagreeable disposition. And here we may observe, that they are such characters as Bruin who bring disrepute on a whole tribe; for we are too apt to form our opinions of a nation by the few individuals we may happen to fall in with, although, probably, no conclusions can be falser. Let us, therefore, be careful ere we form our judgments, and let us not believe that all Bruin's kindred and compatriots were sulky and ill-tempered because he himself was such a disagreeable lump of a bear.

TOWN LIFE.

Bruin woke up next morning with so uncomfortable a feeling of soreness from the rough treatment he had received, that it was with some difficulty he was enabled to move his heavy limbs; and he found sitting so unpleasant a posture, that he lay stretched across two or three branches for several hours, and in a very ill-humour, indeed, watched the activity displayed beneath and around him. Now a stealthy fox, upon some foraging expedition, would come creeping along, his foot-fall scarcely heard on the withered leaves and dead branches; now a timid mouse would leap nimbly by, and, at the least signal of danger, would disappear as if by enchantment; then a frolicsome squirrel, vaulting as fearlessly from bough to bough as if he were not fifty feet from the ground, would arouse him for a minute from his sulky mood, and light up his fierce eye with an expression of interest which it was very clear had no higher source than a hope that the little tumbler might fall down and break his neck, for daring to be in such a good humour. But the birds, above all, excited his anger; for seeing them flying about gaily in the sun, which tinged the tops of the trees so gloriously, Bruin actually growled with indignation—a sound which nearly caused that accident to Master Squirrel that our ungracious hero had desired for him, so terribly was he frightened.

A few days thus spent sufficiently recovered him to render him capable of moving, when he descended from his temporary hospital, and, with the aid of a thick staff, which he had provided himself for the purpose, set off once more, supplying his wants in the way of food with such edibles as fell in his way, a bear not being remarkably particular concerning its quality or kind. One only thought now possessed him,—that of quitting the wooded ground where his life had hitherto been passed, and reaching one of those spots where, as he had heard his parents relate, animals of various kinds congregate together, and live in habitations raised by their own ingenuity; in fact, a city.

"At least," he thought, "if what I have heard of such places be true, and that merit of every kind is certain there to meet its reward, and be properly appreciated, I shall stand a better chance than my neighbours." With this reflection, he shuffled on a little quicker; and the reader, who has been thus allowed a private view of his motives, will observe that modesty was not among Bruin's list of virtues.

After a day's march, with sundry restings by the way—for he was not in good travelling order—he reached the outskirts of the wood; and when he got beyond it, he stood still to mark the prospect, which was, in sooth, a very charming one, and the more striking to him as being so entirely novel. As he stood on a rising ground, the scene lay beneath; and the sun, which was nearing the horizon, darted his level beams through a gentle mist that was beginning to rise from the valley, and made a wondrous golden haze, shedding beauty over every object within its influence. A silvery brook ran from some distant hills, and, after numerous windings, spread into a broad pond; then narrowing again, with an abrupt fall or two, which made its pace the faster, it ran noiselessly through some green meadows, where cattle and horses were grazing, then made a bend into the wood, where it was lost to view. Bruin's quick eye scarcely, however, watched its course, for his whole attention was rivetted on what to him was of more interest,—the city to which his weary steps were directed. It stood upon the margin of the rivulet, just before its waters expanded into the little lake, and seemed to occupy a considerable extent of ground. It was neither handsomely nor regularly built, yet it had an imposing effect as a whole, and in Bruin's eyes seemed to need nothing in the way of architecture. Its inhabitants, I may observe in passing, were principally descendants of canine tribes, with a few pussies, who, for some worldly advantage, had overcome their prejudices to such society; and a flock or two of birds: as the latter, however, were of a volatile disposition, and were constantly on the move, they resided principally in the higher portions of the city, so that they might come and go without interfering with the steadier habits of the animal population. Several horses and black cattle resided in the environs, but, with the exception of a donkey or two, rarely entered the town, for they found few inducements in the noisy streets to compensate them for the charm and tranquillity of a rural life.

After contemplating the scene for some time, Bruin slowly descended the hill, his confidence in his own powers somewhat weakened now he was in sight of the spot where they were to be called into action; one reason for this slight depression of his spirits arising, probably, from his ignorance of the dwellers in the great city, for the intelligence just communicated to the reader was at that time totally unknown to him. The strange appearance, also, of every creature he now met, contributed to abash him; for every one who had any pretensions to respectability wore over the coats with which nature had provided them, clothes of a cut that looked wonderful in the eyes of the untutored Bruin. His own aspect was, meanwhile, not less odd in the opinion of the more civilised animals. His untrimmed hair and beard, his ragged coat, his queer gait, and the unrestrained gape of wonder with which he stared around him, were sufficient to excite the attention of the most indifferent, and it was with a tolerably large train at his heels that he reached the entrance to the principal street. Here crowds of well-dressed dogs, both male and female (the latter always well-attended), were walking about or idling the time away; town-bred puppies, with insolent stare, were lounging at every turn, their delicate paws proving how little they were used to labour. On one side Bruin observed a gracefully-proportioned white cat, veiled, gliding demurely along, whilst a strong tabby, her nurse, purred behind, with three little kittens in her arms, mewing to their hearts' content; and on the other several huge mastiffs, stalking gravely in a row, like policemen in our London streets going to their beats, the animals to which they have been compared being bound on a similar errand.

These various sights proved to Bruin that there must be a different agency at work to that which existed in his native forest. He was wise enough to perceive that mere animal force was not likely to succeed here, or hold the same position as it did in the land where he was born and had spent his earlier years. The appearances of wealth on one hand, the evidences of a soldier-like discipline and order on the other, convinced him that this was no place to vent his ill-humour by an exhibition of brute strength, for that it was sure to meet more than its match; whilst the uncertainty of the punishment which would attend such outbreak, provided it were indulged in, made him resolve, at least, to put a curb upon his public conduct. This was the first great step in Bruin's education; a step, alas! merely taught him by his fears. Had it sprung from higher sources, there would have been a chance of its doing permanent good; but what solid benefit can be reckoned on or attained which arises from such a motive?

The attention that the rough stranger from a distant country met with from the civilised population of Caneville (for that, or something like it, was the name of the city), was beginning to be rather irksome to him. Every lady-dog, as she passed him, seemed anxious to allow him plenty of room; the three kittens in arms, at sight of him set up a chorus of cries, which their nurse tried in vain to appease; a mastiff, who was on guard on the opposite side of the way, seemed very much inclined to interfere for the preservation of public peace; whilst a couple of puppies, touched off in the extreme of the then prevailing fashion at Caneville, turned up their noses and their tails in a way which seemed to render it perfectly marvellous how they kept upon their legs. All this was sufficiently irritating, even to the most good-natured of beings, and Bruin found it especially hard to bear; he was assisted, however, in his prudential resolution to abstain from any outward exhibition of wrath by a sound which was as new to his ear as it was exciting to his feelings. It came from the upper end of the street, where a crowd had assembled; and as every one in his neighbourhood seemed to think the amusement it promised would be of a more interesting kind than baiting a bear, and had hastened in the direction whence it proceeded, Bruin thought he could not do better than follow their example.

On reaching the spot, his great height enabled him to get a view of what was going on; and as he pressed forward, the animals with which he came in contact gladly made way at his approach, so that in a few seconds he stood in the front row of a large circle, the centre of which was occupied by a fat, overgrown pig, with an astonishingly long snout, and a couple of rings through it by way of ornament; two equally long ears, that had evidently been submitted to some curious operation, for they were slit in various places, and hung down from his head like uncombed locks of hair; and a pair of very sharp little eyes, which seemed to have the unpleasant power of piercing right through you, if in their incessant wanderings they chanced to catch a look from your own. It was very evident that this animal, who was quite a *savant*, or, as we should say, a learned pig, enjoyed a high reputation in the community of Caneville, where he had been settled some time; and whenever, as now, he chose to make an outdoor exhibition of himself and his powers, he was certain of a very full audience.

Behind him stood a punchy little bull-dog, with an inflamed countenance, evidently caused by too close application to a mouth-organ, arranged in such a way as to be at a convenient distance from his capacious muzzle; and before him was a drum, an article on which Bruin looked with a curious and most ludicrous expression of physiognomy. As he was now in the foremost van, he gradually edged near and nearer to the object of his attraction, whilst the learned beast was making preparations for a grand display; and just as Bruin had reached the place where the drummer had taken his stand, Herr Schwein (so was he called) gave orders for a flourish of music by way of opening the performance. But how describe the effect which the sound produced on our bear? At the first stroke of the stick on the drum, he leaped from the ground as if he had been shot; then giving utterance to a prolonged howl, he began dancing about in a way which would have been irresistibly funny, if the audience had not been too frightened to stop and witness it. As it happened, a general panic seized the multitude, and off went good part of the population of Caneville, howling, screaming, and yelping to their various homes, where they, of course, each gave a different version of the story. The learned pig alone, and his faithful Tom, who would not run away for any body, were the only creatures who stood their ground; the former, because he had travelled much and was acquainted with the peculiarities of bears; and the latter, partly for the reason just given, and in part because he was so fixed to the drum that to go away without it was impossible; and to go away with it, without previous packing, would have been equally difficult, so he stood his ground and watched the proceedings.

On the ceasing of the music and dispersing of the crowd our hero also stood still, as much surprised as any of the former spectators at the effect he had produced; and then feeling still more sensibly the effects of his fatigues, he sat down panting and exhausted. The pig, who had been quietly watching him, and had evidently been revolving some interesting thoughts in his contemplative brain, shortly after rose, and gathering up the things which were to have figured in his evening's performance, and assisting to pack the drum comfortably on Tom's back, beckoned to the bear, and waddled gently off in an opposite direction of the city to that where Bruin had entered. Our interesting brute hesitated a moment; but being nudged by Tom, who uttered at the same time a word or two of encouragement, which, to render intelligible, may be translated by "Come along, stupid!" he mechanically followed this fast young dog, and they all reached the pig's habitation just as evening was falling.

After the bear had been regaled with a most hearty supper—for pigs, it may be remarked by the way, are famous caterers—his learned host unfolded to him his plans. He explained the nature of his own avocations; how that he had supported himself, and saved a nice little store besides, through telling the fortunes and relating the age of the lady-dogs and doglets of Caneville; and how he performed sundry conjuring tricks, which, though easy enough when found out, had earned for him an astonishing reputation among the simple animals of the city, who never *had* penetrated the secret. He explained, besides, that there were many more he could perform if his figure were more slim and his movements as active as they had been some years ago, before time, by increasing his rotundity, had lessened the ease of his motions; but that if Bruin would undertake to learn them, his fortune was as good as made: for he, Herr Schwein, would not only teach him all he knew, but would reward him with half the profits derived from his performance, when he should have mastered his studies. This proposal so jumped with Bruin's humour, that he consented without further solicitation, and it was agreed that his engagement should commence from the following day.

With the morning's sun did our hero's lessons begin; and as Nature had not added stupidity to his various weaknesses, he made really rapid progress. But poor Piggy found it dreadfully hard work, and more than once repented his bargain; for though reflection and circumstances had made him a philosopher, and travelling had taught him experience, it required all his philosophy and his utmost skill to support the weight of Bruin's unhandsome temper and prevent an utter breach between them. Pride, however, and a natural wish to reap the harvest which he had sown at the cost of so much pains and labour, induced him to persevere, and the day at length arrived when Bruin was to make his next appearance in public. Since the first evening of his arrival he had kept strictly within his employer's grounds, and had familiarised his mind with the mouth-organ and the drum. But now the sun had risen that was to shine on him again abroad; he felt considerably elated; the idea of sporting a handsome pair of silk drawers, and a medal with a ribbon round his neck, and a silver anklet, contributing not a little to produce the feeling.

The pig, who knew the value of notoriety in such cases, had, from early morning, kept Tom parading the streets with a large placard over his shoulders, announcing

THE ARRIVAL
of a
DISTINGUISHED FOREIGNER!
ENGAGED BY HERR SCHWEIN AT A RUINOUS EXPENSE!!
FOR A LIMITED NUMBER OF REPRESENTATIONS,
to perform
HIS EXTRAORDINARY AND INTENSELY INTERESTING
FEATS
before the

HIGHLY-DISCRIMINATING PUBLIC
OF CANEVILLE!!!

The highly-discriminating being thus prepared, assembled in the great square, the place chosen for the exhibition, long before the appointed hour. The ladies were arranged in the foremost rank, with a politeness that was perfectly edifying, whilst knots of fashionable dogs and cats got as near as possible to the reigning favourites; curs of inferior degree occupied the outermost ranks, and a bird or two got gallery places above the heads of the animal spectators. It was when expectation was raised to that pitch which usually finds vent in the most discordant cries, that Bruin, carrying a bag, followed by Tom with the drum, made his appearance,—a sight which caused universal approbation. Some praised his evident strength, others admired his dress, and some again criticised his figure; but when he drew out from his bag a quantity of singular objects, and Tom struck up an extraordinary extempore air with variations on the pipes, accompanied by sundry vicious blows on the drum, public curiosity was strained to the utmost.

MAKING AN IMPRESSION.

When the music ceased, Bruin imperatively waved the spectators back, and the performance began. He handled a pair of knives in a way which made the beholders tremble; for those implements were swallowed and appeared again at the tips of his paws or the end of his nose, without doing him any injury, and they were forced into his arms and drawn furiously across his throat without causing the slightest wound; and then they were tucked into his waistband, and after sundry contortions and leaps, and affected attitudes, they were pulled from out his capacious jaws, where they had stuck fast, to the wonder and delight of the spectators. Then he took up three balls of polished brass, which seemed too heavy for any fashionable puppy present to lift, and commenced a wonderful series of exploits with them. Now they leaped a great height into the air, one after another, with a rapidity which made the crowd's eyes water; then they ran over his shoulders, and down his back, and between his legs, and over his shoulders again in a continuous stream; and then they went bumping over every projecting part of his body, leaping here, jumping there, now on the top of his head, now on the tip of his nose, and never falling to the ground, and always going this game with such wondrous swiftness, as though there were thirty balls instead of three. But the feat which pleased them most, and which may be called the crowning effort of the display, was when Bruin balanced a short stick on his forehead with a pewter plate on the top of it, which, by some mysterious agency, was made to spin round and round, and dazzle the optics of the crowd as it glittered in the sun. At this marvellous sight there was a burst of admiration! Tom blew at his pipes and hammered at his drum with the utmost energy. Two well-dressed young dogs, who had been paying particular attention to a tall young lady with a long sentimental nose, over which a veil dropped gracefully (she was evidently one of the aristocratic greyhound family), gaped with wonder as they stared at the whirling pewter; the young lady herself looked on with a gaze where surprise and admiration were singularly mingled; and the curs, who are less accustomed to restrain their feelings, gave vent to them in vigorous howls. The success was, indeed, complete; and when Tom went round with the plate, a rich harvest amply repaid the pains which had been bestowed on the rehearsals.

PROSPERITY.

Herr Schwein, that very learned pig, who had stationed himself in an unobserved corner of the throng, in order that he might witness the behaviour of his pupil, was delighted, though not astonished, at his success, and gave vent to his feelings in as marked a manner as a philosopher and an animal of his peculiar temperament could be expected to betray. He even went so far as to beg Bruin to embrace him—an experiment he was not likely to desire repeated, for that malicious beast gave him so severe a squeeze, as to cause him an indigestion for several days after. Piggy's calculations, and the joy which he built on them, would not have been of so solid a kind, if he had known a little more of Bruin's disposition; but, though an animal of experience and knowledge of the world, he was in this case too blinded by his pride to form his usually correct judgment. He only considered what the bear owed to him in the way of gratitude for clothing, feeding, and civilising; he grunted with satisfaction as he revolved in his thoughts the goodly treasure which Bruin might be the means of his acquiring; for, philosopher and animal of the world as he was, he had not been able to divest himself of two grand vices,—gluttony and avarice. The former belonged to his tribe, the latter to himself; and though at first sight they would seem in contradiction with each other, he managed somehow to permit, in his own proper person, that both should have equal sway; and the older he grew, the larger and firmer-rooted did these two passions become. He was getting also so unwieldy, that indolence was, to a certain extent, forced upon him; and this was another powerful consideration which induced him to look on the accession of Bruin as a real benefit.

Unhappy, however, the lot of that animal who should repose any degree of confidence in good to be derived from such a temper and disposition! As day by day developed some new feature which helped to betray a character singularly unamiable and unattractive, so day by day did Herr Schwein's habitation resound with growls and grunts of anger, where formerly reigned the completest calm. Bruin's performances also lacking novelty, began to pall upon the public taste; and though Tom trudged about with his placards more vigorously than ever, and wore the soles of his poor paws thin with the exercise, the novelty was dying out, and the fashionable puppies began to be witty in their whispered remarks upon the person of the bearer. The bear had got a great deal too lazy to learn any fresh exploits; and the pig, indeed, was almost too much out of spirits to teach them. Besides this, Bruin had acquired habits of rather an expensive kind, to indulge which required a good deal of money; and, as Herr Schwein suspected that his due half of the now diminished receipts was withheld from him, quarrels not unnaturally ensued.

These various annoyances produced a great change in poor Piggy, who, perhaps, felt more deeply the overthrow of his pet projects, than the actual loss his bargain had entailed on him; though the loss itself was not trifling, for Bruin's enormous appetite, which he indulged to a frightful extent, went considerably beyond the income that his diminished exertions produced, and there was a chance, as matters stood, that this resource would soon fail altogether. It is not surprising, then, if the Herr should contemplate breaking off his engagement, and terminating at once the difficulties which seemed to threaten him, by turning the great bear adrift upon the world. But a stronger power than a pig's was about to settle the question, a power to which all animals are equally amenable: and thus was it brought into action.

It was evening; Bruin and Tom, the former in excessively ill-humour, the latter much as usual, though sulky, returned home, where the Herr awaited them with impatience. It did not require a very great amount of sagacity to learn that they had been unsuccessful, for disappointment was plainly visible on the features of both. From Bruin nothing could be obtained in the way of information, for he had thrown himself on the ground, and stuffed his wide jaws with some delicacies Piggy had reserved for his own supper, so it was to Tom his master's eyes were directed for an explanation. Now that valuable servant's *fort*, never lay in making an eloquent discourse, or even in describing the most ordinary facts in a plain and intelligible manner; and in this instance, as his feelings interfered with the relation of facts, a tolerably large stock of patience, and some cleverness to boot, were needed to understand the account.

This was, after cross-examination, what Herr Schwein managed to comprehend. They had gone to the marketplace as usual, and, to their delight, found it crowded, immediately jumping to the conclusion that the public mind of Caneville was not so utterly degraded as they had begun to fancy it. The innocent conjecture was soon, however, disabused; for on their drawing nearer they observed that faithless population gathered about "Another Distinguished Foreigner," with a remarkably long beard and a fierce pair of horns, who proclaimed himself a magician from beyond the land where the sun rose, and rejoiced in the name of Doctor Capricornus, A.V.G.T., and M.U.H.S., which the great learning of Herr Schwein interpreted by A Very Great Traveller, or Thief, and Member of the Universal Herbage or Humbug Society. Now, the feats displayed by this new candidate for public favour were of the stupidest order (remember, this is not the statement of a disinterested party), consisting merely in pointing out any pebble on the ground that any one of the crowd should have previously fixed on, and mounting to the top of a little ladder and balancing himself on the tips of his horns at the upper round; yet it was enough to excite the enthusiasm of the lookers-on: nor could all the cries of Bruin, bidding them come and see what true genius really was; nor all the dulcet notes of Tom, though he blew at his pipes till he was black in the face, and thrashed his drum till he beat in its crown, procure them a single spectator. Thoroughly disgusted, they quitted the spot and returned home, Bruin getting into a dispute with one of the City police by the way for comporting himself bearishly towards a richly-dressed and genteel-looking cat, who was quietly serenading his mistress, seated at a balcony.

As Tom finished his relation, a slight squeak issued from the pig's throat, but from its profoundest depths, as if it came from the bottom of his heart. Once or twice, indeed, he turned his snout to the place where the bear, who had finished his employer's supper, lay at his full length asleep, as though he intended to arouse him; but his philosophy or his physical weakness made him change his resolution, and, making a motion to Tom to lend him some assistance, he tottered off with difficulty to bed, where he cast himself down as if he were tired of the world and its struggles. At least his manner so far affected Tom that he could not prevail on himself to quit his master's side; but after watching him with interest for a full hour, and observing him in a deep sleep, he stretched his body upon some clean straw, instead of seeking his own crib, and was soon likewise in a state of forgetfulness.

It must have been about midnight that Tom was aroused by a suppressed grunting; he started up, and, by the aid of the moon, beheld Herr Schwein lying on his back, and convulsively kicking his legs in the air. He ran to his head and tried to raise him up, but his weight was more than he could manage, so he called out in his loudest voice for the assistance of Bruin. That ungracious beast, however, though waked by the noise, felt no inclination to have his repose disturbed; so bid him hold his peace, and let honest folks go to sleep. Tom was a thoroughly faithful creature at heart, though a rough and untutored one. The want of feeling displayed by the bear, and his ingratitude in thus allowing his master to struggle without even lending him a paw, aroused all the indignation of his honest nature; so, flying at Master Bruin, he caught hold of the tip of his ear and bit it till the great beast roared with pain, and, effectually roused, followed his adversary about the place in order to punish him for his insolence. In his awkward evolutions he caught one of his legs in a heap of straw, and fell full sprawl over poor Herr Schwein. A small grunt, like a sigh with a bad cold, escaped the learned Pig: it was his last! for, when Bruin raised himself up, he found his late employer perfectly motionless; nor did all his efforts, such as pulling his snout, and shaking his trotters, and twisting his tail, succeed in producing the slightest impression. The bear was puzzled. He squatted down beside his old master, and, sucking his right paw, whilst he scratched his pate with his left, gazed long at the prostrate body. Meanwhile Tom drew nigh, and guessing at the truth from his companion's attitude and the pig's breathless quiet, raised his nose to the roof of the dwelling and uttered a long and dismal howl of sorrow. Again and again, at brief intervals, did the faithful servant thus deplore his master's fate, till Bruin, angered by the noise, threw the broken drum at the unconscious mourner, with such effect, indeed, that the shattered extremity alighted on his crown, and for the time completely buried him, his voice sounding singularly sepulchral from the depths of the hollow instrument. It effectually stopped the current of his grief by creating a flood of irritation, which only respect for the dead prevented his giving vent to, for he would otherwise have little heeded either the strength or ferocity of his antagonist.

Bruin, who had betrayed no feeling of any kind at the sight of his late benefactor thus converted into pork, now returned to his own bed, and was soon again in a comfortable snore; but the faithful

Tom still sat beside the body of his master, and patiently watched there till daylight.

The sun rose, and many neighbours, apprised of the event, made their appearance; some urged by curiosity to see how a dead pig looked, some stimulated by avarice, hoping there might be a trifle or two to pick up, and a few from a higher motive—the wish, namely, to show respect for the memory of the deceased, by assisting, if necessary, his survivors. Herr Schwein, however, had come amongst them alone, nor was it thought that he had kith or kin; for no mention of any amiable *frau*, or sow, no syllable of any interesting piglet, had ever issued from his learned jaws. He died as he had lived, among strangers; and, alas! all the learning he had acquired was destined to perish with him: for, with one exception, Herr Schwein had never committed any of his thoughts or experiences to writing. I have said, with *one* exception; for the occasion is worth noting, as it was on a matter interesting, indeed, to every epicure in the universe. The subject which then engaged his pen bore the following title:—"*Signs by which the most unobservant may detect in the soils of the world the existence of Truffles; together with an Essay on the most effectual mode of cultivating them.*" And it may well be conjectured, from the great learning and fitness of the writer to deal with such a subject, how much new light must have been thrown upon it. Unfortunately for the tribes of gourmands, and poor Piggy's fame, this valuable paper was never destined to electrify the world; for, cast into the street by Bruin among other articles, considered, alas! of no value, it was picked up by some ignorant puppy passing by, who, seeing it written in German character, and not understanding a word of it, tore up the priceless document to make lights for his cigars.

Two mastiffs, who had been informed of the death, kept watch meanwhile without the house; and when night again came on they were joined by a couple of ugly curs, whose business it was to convey the body to its last resting-place without the city; for the dogs, with great good sense, had an intense dislike to bury the dead among the living. The mortal remains of Herr Schwein being placed upon a kind of sledge, were drawn slowly down to the little lake, followed by Tom, as chief and only mourner, for Bruin was so devoid of feeling as to refuse even this last tribute to the memory of one who had been his best friend; and when the funeral procession reached the water, the body was gently let down into the current, which bore it gradually away. Poor Tom sent after it a prolonged and melancholy howl, the last sad adieu of a simple but faithful heart; and then turning his steps, which were mechanically leading him towards his late home, in quite an opposite direction, he set off upon a lonely pilgrimage, resolving in his own mind that many a scene should be traversed ere he again gazed on his native city of Caneville.

Meanwhile Bruin, who felt not the least alarm at Tom's continued absence, found himself suddenly in a position of the highest prosperity. As no one was there to claim the property of the deceased, he took possession of it as his right. Every corner was ransacked, every hiding-place examined, and a large store of costumes, and things of every kind, gathered in the course of the late Herr's wanderings in different lands, were dragged from their obscurity.

A VERY GREAT BEAR.

His present habitation did not, however, suit his change of fortune: he must have a house in the most fashionable quarter of the town. When this was obtained, not satisfied with the simple name his fathers had honestly borne for so many generations, he resolved to dub himself a nobleman, which he could the more easily do in a place where his connexions were unknown, so styled himself Count von Bruin forthwith. The wardrobe of his late learned employer furnished him with a suit of astonishingly fine clothes, which fitted him to a nicety; so on every fine morning, dressed therein, with hat cocked upon his crown, his paws grasping a cane, and placed under his coat-tails, so as to show off all the glory of his waistcoat, frill, and splendid jewellery, he marched into the streets. He made so imposing a figure in his new dress, and assumed such an air of pomposity, that it was no wonder the uninitiated should have been deceived, and have taken him for a lion of the very first nobility; nor can we be surprised that a poor cur, almost in a state of nudity, should, in the most abject manner, supplicate a trifle from "His Lordship;" that an ignorant cat, in passing, should take off his cap and make a profound bow; or a kitten, just behind, cross its paws as though it stood in the presence of a superior. There was one, however, who penetrated through all his disguise; one who had watched him with interest when he made his *debut* in the public square and drew down such abundant admiration, and who, by some feeling for which she could not account, had followed his varying fortunes till she saw him thus rich, superbly dressed, and strutting down the street, as though Caneville were too small to hold him,—and that one was the Hon. Miss Greyhound.

REVERSES.

Solitary as were Bruin's habits by nature, he had felt, since his residence in a town, a change stealing gradually over him, and the necessity of companionship becoming every day more sensibly experienced. In his late position, he had had the constant companionship of Tom and the learned society of his master, which, indeed, he was but little capable of appreciating, besides the acquaintance of some inferior animals whom he had managed to fall in with during his idle hours; though that these must have been of the very lowest class, the reader, who is aware of the character of that great beast, will readily suppose. Tom was, however, now gone; poor Schwein, too, had departed; and Bruin's fine clothes and altered condition entirely precluded at present a return to his former associates. Society, he felt, he must have, and upon his choice now depended his future fortunes. It was whilst this necessity was pressing on his brain that one morning, when lolling in all the indolence of ignorance allied to wealth, he was surprised at the appearance of a diminutive spaniel, admitted by his porter, who, dressed in a rich scarlet livery, bore a letter in his belt, which he presented with a certain fawning grace to our hero, and hastily departed. This was the first epistle that worthy had ever held in his own paws, so it may well be judged he was but little prepared to investigate its contents. He turned it over and over, and then put it to his nose, for the scent which it emitted was pleasant to his sense of smell; but still this gave him no hint at its meaning. Never before had he felt the annoyance which a want of education inevitably causes; but now that it did strike him, instead of arousing his energies to cure so serious a defect,—a cure, too, which he could under present circumstances so easily accomplish,—it only moved his anger to think that the little scrap of paper which he held in his paw, and which he could without the slightest effort crush into nothingness, withheld its secrets from him, whilst every mincing puppy in the streets could command its every word. Ah, Master Bruin! Master Bruin! you are not the first to make the discovery that knowledge is superior to brute force. Angry or not, he wished to know the meaning of the note; and summoning to his presence one who had managed to procure the chief place in his household, cunning Fox as he was, he commanded that worthy to read its contents aloud. Fox obeyed, not at all displeased that he should be selected for this duty, as he foresaw, from the so-called Count's ignorance, that he would be able at a future period to turn his intimate knowledge of his master's secrets to good account. He, therefore, read as follows:—

"You may believe I must be actuated by a strong feeling in your favour, when I thus forget what is due to my sex and rank, and overcome all the prejudices which canine society builds up as a barrier to intercourse with foreigners. I confess it; the feeling *is* a strong one: but I rely on your honour to save me from the ill effects my imprudence might otherwise lay me open to. If you are willing to know farther, and are the animal I take you for, you will be in waiting tomorrow evening after sunset, at the extremity of the mews in the cats' quarter of the city."

This missive, written in bold but feminine characters, was without a signature; and when Fox had retired, with a cunning leer upon his sharp features, and Bruin was left alone to meditate upon the singularity of the adventure, that great beast lost himself in conjectures as to the writer, and figured to his imagination a creature very different, no doubt, to the being actually in question. His impatience, however, to get over the interval of time which must elapse ere his curiosity could be gratified, was sensibly felt by every inmate of the mansion. Nothing seemed to go right; the soup was tasteless, the viands were overdone, and the vegetables raw. Never was there so fastidious a bear; the cook more than once contemplated some rash act; the poor little turnspits crept into corners with their tails between their legs, fully expecting to be sacrificed in some moment of wrath; whilst the various house-servants, pussies of doubtful reputation, seemed to creep about the place as though they were every moment in dread of being accused of purloining certain savoury made-dishes, reserved especially for cook's private friends. Fox, too, the steward and factotum of the establishment, appeared not to possess his usual sleek and quiet ease, but, as the evening drew near, got restless and fidgetty, though he tried to be calm, and even more jocose than usual. He had been absent half the morning, no one knew for what purpose; not that he ever condescended to divulge the causes of his movements, but there was a slyer look in his eyes, and a sharper appearance about his clever, pointed nose, than ordinarily animated those features.

The hour drew nigh. The sun was going down when the Count von Bruin, most superbly dressed, sallied forth from his dwelling. His demeanour was observed and criticised by every domestic in his household, who, crowding to the windows, watched that great bear go forth,—as he fancied, to conquer. Fox allowed him to turn the corner; then, enveloped in a cloak which completely hid his figure, he let himself out and glided after his master.

Bruin, meanwhile, strutted on till he reached the quarter of the city inhabited by the descendants of the feline race; and as he had never before been in that part of the town, he was at first utterly confounded by the discordant cries. Instead, too, of the order prevailing in the canine portions, the inhabitants seemed to take delight in the wildest gymnastic demonstrations, and certainly seemed to prefer the house-tops to any other lounging-place. Kittens, in horrible abundance, were frisking about in every direction, and the scene was altogether of a character which seemed to justify the wisdom of the magnates of Caneville in obliging this singular people to dwell in a distinct part of the town; a rule which, with a few exceptions, was strictly carried out.

On reaching the mews, a place so called at the outskirts of the city in this direction, and sufficiently removed from the noisy streets as to make the spot a very solitary one, Bruin perceived he was alone at the rendezvous; so, to while away the time, he strutted to and fro, and meditated, in his usual style, on his own self-importance. He was aroused from his reverie by a slight bark, or cough; and raising his head, he perceived in the dim light a tall and graceful figure deeply veiled.

He hastily advanced, his rough nature for the first time touched at this proof of confidence, and his vanity suddenly rising to a dangerous height, and taking the delicate white paw, which drooped gracefully from a mantle, within his own, he unclosed his jaws to make some tender speech. But before he had time to commit himself by his ignorance, the young lady uttered an aristocratic squeak, and darted away with the utmost swiftness, and Bruin at the same instant found himself seized by a strong grip from behind. He turned round with a violence which threw his assailant a dozen paces off, into a pool of stagnant water, his own coat being slit right up the back by the movement; but he was at once attacked by half-a-dozen others, who seemed bent on his destruction. Bruin's great strength, however, served him in good stead; with his back against an old wall, he received the assaults of his adversaries with all his wonted ferocity: so that after ten minutes' fighting they drew off, leaving two of their number motionless on the ground, and a third struggling in vain to escape from the unsavoury hole where the whisk of Bruin's coat-tails had cast him. To this spot Bruin now proceeded; and sitting himself down on the edge, told the struggling dog he would help him out if he would divulge the meaning of this unexpected attack on him.

The half-drowned cur, having supplicated the bear in vain to let him out before he commenced his narration, in accents sadly interrupted by his throat getting at intervals choked with dirty water, explained that himself and the others of his assailants were the attendants of one of the most noble families in Caneville; and that their master, learning from some member of Count von Bruin's household that he (the Count) intended meeting the eldest daughter at this spot to-night, had commanded a body of his servitors to be in readiness to fall upon him, and if possible take him prisoner, for presuming to raise or lower his eyes to a damsel of such standing.

Scarcely had Bruin heard this communication to an end, than, despite his promise and the poor dog's cries, he caught up a huge clod of earth and dropped it upon the devoted head of the struggling animal beneath. There was a great splash; a bubble or two came to the surface of the horrid pool, and the brutal deed was consummated. Yet at the same moment Bruin regretted he had been so precipitate, for he had not learnt *which* member of his household had played the spy. As he slowly left the place, he revolved this subject in his mind, but could come to no satisfactory conclusion; for though Fox appeared the most likely to be guilty, that worthy animal had made himself so useful to his master, that he could not well manage without him. He resolved, nevertheless, to watch him closely, and with this prudent resolve he reached his own door.

Very different was his appearance now to that which it presented on his issuing from the mansion. His coat torn to ribbons, his hat without a crown, his majestic frill rumpled and bloody, and his waistcoat without a single button left wherewith to restrain the exuberance of his linen. All his domestics were eager in their inquiries and offers of service; and Fox was so overpowering in his expressions of regret, that all suspicion vanished from Bruin's brain at once; and he attributed his informant's tale to some malicious calumny, invented to save his life and conceal the true cause of the attack upon him.

Our hero, finding that the paths of gallantry were filled with so much unpleasantness, resolved, like a prudent animal, to avoid them carefully in future; but as his desire for an introduction to society continued, he availed himself of the offer of his steward, who promised to procure him introductions to youth of the best families. The class with which Fox managed to bring him into connexion was the most worthless in Caneville, consisting of fast young dogs, who had a singular knack of reversing the order of nature, and going to bed when other animals were getting up, and thinking of rising when the discreet part of the world deemed it time to retire to rest. They had formed themselves into a sort of club, which they called the "Hard and Fast;" and, indeed, no terms could better express the habits of the members; for they gamed hard, drank hard, and talked hard, and lived so uncommonly *fast*, that it was not surprising that, though quite young, they should have many of the infirmities of age. To these worthies Bruin was an acquisition; for he was rich, ignorant, and gullible, whilst they were poor, grasping, and unscrupulous. At the very first interview, all parties were equally delighted with each other; the ease of his new companions' manners was perfectly charming to Bruin, who considered it as a proof of their breeding, and every following day strengthened the connexion. Riotous parties of pleasure were constantly projected, for which their friend Von Bruin paid; banquets of the most expensive kind were always spread upon his table, at which his "dear fellows of the club" assisted—themselves; and, indeed, so closely were the bonds of union drawn, that after some time many of them could not bear to separate from their esteemed Count; and, therefore, took up their residence with him altogether.

If disorder were running such a race in company with the chief of the establishment, it may be conjectured that but little prudence or economy was displayed by the domestics. Extravagance of every kind ran riot amongst them as wildly as with their master, and they scrupled not at all sorts of petty pilfering, where there were none to censure or restrain. Fox, it is true, had the right, and possessed the influence requisite to do so; but, for some evil design of his own, possibly that his private peccadilloes might escape unnoticed, he seemed tacitly to submit to such a state of things, and in some instances actually encouraged it. And what could be the only result of such a life of dissipation, unchecked by a single effort of discretion? Why, nothing but the most irretrievable ruin; and ruined the bear was after three months' trial. And when, following a banquet of several days' duration, the clouded intellects of the beast were made sensible of the fact; when he found his table cleared for the last time both of servants and guests; when he traversed the various apartments of his mansion, and observed all stripped, destroyed, and echoing only to the sounds of his own footsteps; when, in fine, he discovered that he was again alone in the world, without any portion of that wealth which he had so sadly abused, and with many new and vicious tastes which he had no longer the means to gratify; bitter, indeed, were his lamentations, shocking his fits of anger. These over, and they lasted long, long days, he seriously examined the state of his affairs. With the exception of the clothes upon his back, and a little change in his pocket, he possessed absolutely nothing, so effectually had his kind friends and faithful servants stripped him of his means: it was, therefore, with no enviable feelings he left the house, his house no longer, to seek a shelter for his head, and a crust to appease his hunger.

He carefully avoided all his former resorts, and directed his steps to those parts of the town where poverty and vice were accustomed to assemble, strong in their numbers and their misery. Among them he now strove to bury his griefs and acquire consolation; but, alas, it was at the cost of every hope of virtue which might yet lurk in his nature! Characters like Bruin's, that are ever more apt to imitate the evil than the good which is around them, can only acquire some fresh stain from every contact with the wicked; and thus our bear sunk lower and lower in the scale of beasts, till many even of his new associates at last shrunk from him.

THROWS A-PENNY.

Some months after Bruin's being turned out of his splendid home there was a great fair held, just without the town of Caneville; and, as is usual in such cases, the lowest orders of the population assembled there. The Hon. Miss Greyhound, who had been a prey to feelings of a very mixed nature since her interrupted interview with Bruin, had joined a party of fashionables in an unusually long walk, and on their return to the city by a different route they came upon the fair. They stopped on a rising ground at some little distance to view the sports; then observing a group with a tall ungainly figure in the centre, a little to the right, they drew nearer to observe the proceedings. The great beast in the centre had his

40

back to them, so they could not observe his features; but they saw that his clothes were ragged, his whole appearance very dirty, and his hat a particularly bad one. A dozen of heavy sticks were at his feet, and a couple were under his arm; whilst at some twenty paces distant two wands, with an ornament or trinket at the top of each, were stuck upright in a straw bag, ready to be thrown at by any adventurous puss or puppy who had a coin at his disposal. A couple of cats were lovingly walking at some distance, another was climbing a large tree which overhung the place, and a fourth was lazily seated high above; whilst, in the neighbourhood of the animal who was presiding over the scene, were several dogs and a cat or two waiting for their turn. The tall beast now altered his position, and the strongly-marked features of a bear became plainly visible to the party; at the same time he caught sight of the fashionable group, and, with a fierce expression in his eye, surlily invited the well-dressed males to take their chance at "Three throws a-penny!"

A gentle howl from Miss G. was the only reply, as the party hastily retreated; for she recognized in the dirty, degraded beast, who was presiding over this vulgar sport, the object she had once looked on with affection, the once wealthy Count von Bruin.

PROGRESS.

The fair of Caneville was like fairs in most other parts of the world, and contained the usual elements of fun and wickedness, toys and dirt, sweets and other messes. As all these various ingredients looked best at night, when the broad sun was withdrawn and an artificial light very feebly supplied its place, it was towards evening that the fair began to fill, and doubtful characters to ply their various vocations. It was matter of remark that there was much more quarrelling and ill-humour in the fair this particular year, than there had been for several previous periods; and it was also observed that a tall and powerful bear—no other than our hero Bruin—was ever in the midst of it, either as an instigator or a principal. This circumstance made the authorities more than usually alert, and caused Master Bruin to be closely watched.

It was at the close of the last day, after many scenes of evil which it is not necessary to describe, that a serious disturbance arose in the part of the field where Bruin had his stand. Blows soon followed angry words; the contending parties flew at each other with great ferocity; growl followed growl, and bite succeeded bite, so that a good deal of blood was shed—ill blood; so, perhaps, better out than in;—and as Bruin's sticks were conveniently at hand as weapons of offence, they were soon seized upon, and used so indiscriminately, that almost every throw told. Many were stretched on the ground, and one of the mastiff-police was thought to be killed. This was a serious offence, indeed, and those who knew the penalty attending such a calamity instantly took to flight. They were as instantly pursued; and when about to be captured, with one voice denounced Bruin as the culprit; though, in fact, it was not he who had struck the blow, and they knew it: but such was his known ferocity and ill-temper, that to shield themselves they were ready to give up the wrong beast, whom no one loved, and whom every one would have suspected as the author of the calamity. So the bear, in spite of his protestations of innocence, and in spite too of a most furious resistance, in the course of which he got more than one savage bite from some small animal he had injured, he was dragged off to prison.

The place used for this purpose was a portion of a ruined castle, standing in the centre of the town, on the banks of the rivulet before spoken of; the ruin itself being of great antiquity, and having been evidently erected by a very different class of beings to that which formed the present population of Caneville. Several compartments were adapted for the purpose, all more or less secure; but the square stone chamber into which Bruin was thrust was the strongest of them all. The door opening outwards was closed on him, and secured by a heavy mass of rock, which the united efforts of several of the police rolled against it; and having thus deposited the prisoner in safety, a couple mounted guard at the entrance, in case by any chance the great strength of the bear should succeed in removing the fastening. Bruin seemed, however, in no humour to make the experiment. Sore and worn out, he crawled into a corner and was soon fast asleep, resuming in his dreams some of his old avocations. He woke at daylight, and immediately rose to examine his prison. The door he sniffed at, but passed by; the window was at so great a height from the floor that he could not reach it upon tiptoe, but he remarked that a very delicious puff of fresh air came down an aperture originally used as a chimney. He moved hastily towards it, and many feet above observed the blue sky, and the large branch of a tree waving over the aperture. Had Messieurs the Police been aware of Bruin's climbing propensities, they would scarcely have left this point unguarded; as it was, the bear proceeded immediately to take advantage of it. With a spring he caught hold of an opening formed by a missing stone, and drawing his body up to his paw, he stuck his foot into the hole and pressed his broad back against the opposite side; a projecting brick gave him a second hold, and then the difficulty was over, for the chimney narrowing he managed to get up by the simple pressure of his knees and back, and the use of his broad and muscular paws. A few seconds sufficed for him to reach the top, on which he sat with his heels dangling in the air, to enjoy the prospect and take breath, while he deliberated on his farther proceedings.

Meanwhile an inquiry had been entered upon by the authorities of Caneville concerning the riot, in which one of the police was alleged to have been killed, but as the object of the inquiry limped into the assembly during the sitting, it was not considered worth while to hear evidence as to the authors of his death; and as he, moreover, distinctly stated that the beast who struck the blow was not a bear, it was ordered that the bear who was in custody on the charge should be liberated forthwith. Great was the surprise of his guards, however, on proceeding to his prison, to find that he had anticipated the verdict and had taken the liberty of setting himself free; in what way was pretty clear, as, on looking up the chimney, they were no less amused than astonished to see him just in the act of swinging himself on to the projecting branch of the tree and disappear from their view. They ran round into the court to mark the end of Bruin's manœuvres, but he had been too quick for them;

not knowing of his being again a free bear, and apprehensive of being pursued, he had descended the tree with the utmost velocity, climbed over a ruined wall, and dropping, not lightly, into the stream, with a few bold strokes reached the opposite shore, where he immediately climbed a leafy oak, with the intention of waiting till the hue and cry was over.

He kept his position very quietly all day, rather surprised that no commotion should be visible in and about the prison, of which he commanded a good view; and as evening was falling he resolved to descend, and, recrossing the stream higher up, seek refuge in some one of his late haunts. Just as he was about putting this resolution into effect he heard voices beneath the tree, and lay quite still to listen. But what was his astonishment, as they drew nearer, to perceive that one of the two foxes from whom the sounds proceeded, was his former steward and factotum! His interest in their movements was of course increased, and he listened, with his ears and eyes bent down, to catch their every syllable and look. The stranger fox, it appeared, was about crossing the brook to the city, and the other one had accompanied him thus far, but refused to enter the town. On this, the following words reached Bruin's ear:—

Stranger.—I have noticed more than once, cousin, that you avoid the town; and yet I have known you to declare that no one but a cow could live in the country.

Fox.—True enough, my dear fellow; but since I left *his* service, you know, I don't care to run the risk of meeting him.

Stranger.—Ha! ha! I see. You are rather apprehensive he should seize you by the throat, and exclaim, "*My* money or *your* life!"

Fox.—Hush! hush! who knows what ears may be listening? Enough that I have a comfortable competency, and don't choose to run the risk of losing it.

Stranger.—Well, well, cousin, I say no more; but remember, your grandfather and mine never left his home for fear of meeting with a wolf who owed him a grudge, and was found dead in his bed, having been murdered by the very wolf after all. Come! you needn't look so down about it, old fellow; nothing half so bad, I hope, will come to you.—Ta! ta!

So saying, the stranger fox took leave of his cousin, and was soon on the opposite shore.

Fox waited till he saw him land, and then slowly turned to retrace his steps.

Scarcely, however, had he taken half-a-dozen paces, than a rushing noise smote his ears; and before he could raise his head a heavy body struck him between the shoulders, with a violence which dashed him flat on to the ground. He neither moved nor uttered a cry: his neck was broken. With a savage howl, Bruin—for it is easy to guess that it was he—put his heavy paw upon the other's chest; but finding all still, he examined his clothes, whence he took all the valuables. He paused in his work to chide his own precipitancy; for had he followed the Fox he might, perhaps, have learnt his dwelling and regained great part of his property. It was too late now; so, giving a savage kick on the face of the unfortunate animal, he heaped it over with leaves, and pursued his original intention of regaining the city, and before night was once more beneath the roof of a late associate.

He remained for several days perfectly quiet and inactive; but finding no search was instituted for him, he, little by little, resumed his old habits, and, as many knew to their cost, his old overbearing temper.

Among the tastes prevailing to an immense extent in the community of Caneville, a great love for those dainties which we call oysters had always been remarkable. It occurred to Bruin, as he had now some trifling capital, that he would invest a portion in such articles as made up the fixtures and stock-in-trade of an oyster-merchant: the former expression is, however, a misnomer, for the stall and tubs included under the term fixtures would be more properly described as moveables. This was soon effected;

and Bruin having chosen a semi-respectable thoroughfare, where he would have a chance of a customer or two from the upper, and would not be too far removed from the lower class of Caneville society, he planted his stall, arranged his tubs, spruced up his own person with the addition of a most formidable collar and a most doubtfully clean apron, and vociferated his "Penny a lot, pups! penny a lot!" in a way which greatly edified the bystanders. The bystanders were, however, soon induced to become purchasers, for very few of them could resist oysters, if they had the wherewithal to purchase them; and Bruin's natives were so fine and fresh, and he had so clever a knack of opening them, that it was really worth the money to see him do that, and many actually went there for the purpose: so that it really seemed he had at last hit upon a business for which he was entirely suited, which met also the public views, and that a short time would enable him, with prudence, to save provision for his old age.

SELLING THE NATIVES.

But, alas, the perversity of bears! No sooner did anything like a smile from Fortune's face alight upon him, than he seemed resolved, by his uncompromising temper, to turn it to a frown! As long as the business was new to him, he took pleasure in performing the duties belonging to it in a proper manner; a little roughly, it may be, but still—properly. Directly it grew familiar, he became careless; and he had a most wilful habit of aggravating his customers, which could not, of course, continue without seriously injuring his trade. For instance, when some pert young puppy would come forward, and civilly enough request his "one or two penn'orth of natives," Bruin would first insist on having the money paid down, and would then tantalise his customer by offering him the opened oyster and hastily withdrawing it just as the impatient jaws were about to close on the desired morsel, and so on to the end, to the vast irritation of many an irascible little animal.

And a day came when this same spirit caused the upset of his trade, and set a veto upon his "selling the natives," at least in Caneville, for the future. A fox and a young terrier had both paid their money, and were eagerly waiting for their oysters, disturbing by their clamour a grave old dog who was licking the shell of his last penn'orth, when a domestic from a wealthy family, arrayed in a superb livery cloak, came up to order a lot for his master. The usual game—if it can be called so, when all the fun was on one side, was being played—three distinct efforts had been made by Terrier to get his second instalment, when, in the struggle which ensued, the vinegar-bottle was knocked over, the cork came out, and the perfidious liquid, highly adulterated with vitriol (for, to their shame be it spoken, the dogs of distillers did not hesitate to endanger the lives of the inhabitants by such practices), poured in full volume over the rich livery-cloak of the servant, which was completely spoiled. The master, who was as powerful as he was avaricious, made a formal complaint against Bruin and his stall as a nuisance; and as it was impossible even in Caneville to obtain perfect justice, the report, without other inquiry, was taken as correct, and Bruin, boiling with rage, had the mortification of seeing his tubs smashed, his stall destroyed, and his "natives" scattered all abroad without being able to strike a blow in their defence.

DOWN HILL.

Bruin, that great animal, was seated on a bank overhanging the river, which, being shallow at this spot, brawled loudly over its pebbly bed, some parts of which were dry. It was at such a distance from the city, that all the noises common to its streets were united into one buzz or hum, and the whole scene was well adapted to suggest meditations upon private matters, or the affairs of the world in general. Yet Bruin did not seem influenced by any such reflections: if one might venture a guess from the appearance of his physiognomy, one would say that nothing in particular occupied his brains; true, his looks were black, his head was cast down, his eyes, as usual, were cunning and ferocious, but then they were always so, and consequently presented no index of what was passing within.

Suddenly his features brightened, his face assumed an expression of interest, and he put his paw gently behind him to secure a stone, whilst his gaze was intently fixed on a dry spot of the bed below. Following the direction of his look, one might have perceived an uncommonly fat frog pulling with all his strength at the leg of another one whose body was hidden behind a heap of pebbles, and certainly the sight was one to amuse a wiser head than a bear's. The standing-place of the paunchy little animal being very green and slippery, and the leg which he so tightly clasped belonging to a fellow creature of no ordinary robustness, the struggle was diversified every few seconds by the fat fellow toppling on to his nose or back, or being dragged behind the heap, and then suddenly reappearing, still holding with passionless determination to that devoted leg, and tumbling about without uttering a syllable. It was when the greater part of his body was exposed to view in a position more comical than dignified, so great were his exertions, that Bruin's stone, cast with unerring aim, descended upon the unfortunate frog. It hit him upon the softest and most projecting part of his back, and had the effect of raising him instantly into a perpendicular position, when looking round and observing the huge beast above about to repeat the application, he clapped his broad hand over the wounded place, and limped hastily away; nor could all the enticements of the bear, conveyed, it is true, in very unflattering language, induce him to expose his person to the chances of a second throw.

Bruin's attention was shortly after aroused anew, by observing a wretched old dog tottering under the weight of a large bundle, strapped upon his back, which he was conveying to the city. He came within a few feet of the bear, whom he knew slightly, and casting down his load, which he seemed to have brought from a distance, wiped his face with his ragged tail. Bruin was the first to speak.

Bruin (with a grunt).—Hard at work as usual, eh! Flip?

Flip.—Yes, Master Bruin, these are hard times; no bone to pick without it, you know.

Bruin (with a very emphatic grunt).—That depends; some have lots of bones, and fine clothes, and warm beds, without doing anything harder for them than picking the one, putting on the other, and sleeping on the third;—but never mind that; what have you got there in your bundle, old fellow?

Flip.—Why, songs, Master Bruin; and you, who are fond of music, might make mints of money by selling 'em, if you'd only choose to do it.

Bruin (pricking up his ears).—Ah, Master Flip! and in what way?

Flip.—Why, here are all the new songs that have been sung for the last ten seasons by the Caterwaullic Society at their new Hall, and a lot more besides, printed in half-a-dozen columns three times as long as my tail, and all for a penny. Why, the very names of them are worth double the money. I'm going to take this package to old Powtry the bookseller, and, if you're in want of a job, I'll recommend you to him as one of the venders.

CHEAP HARMONY.

The proposal in Bruin's state of finance was not to be despised, for since his forced retirement from business, he had found his stomach and his pockets, by a very natural sympathy, suffering from precisely the same complaint—a degree of emptiness, namely—which there seemed no chance of finding a remedy for; but he had sundry doubts as to his capabilities for the new employment he was about seeking, particularly as he was aware his reputation was more notorious than favourable. To his surprise, however, though his person was well known to the individual Powtry, not the slightest objection seemed to be made on the score of anything. The terms of his agreement, alas! not remarkably liberal, were arranged; Bruin spent a couple of days in conning over his task, and forgetting to thank the poor dog who had procured him his situation, he once more entered the busy streets of Caneville to add his bass voice to the other cries of that populous city. His appearance, as he made his way into the centre of the most active thoroughfare, holding in one paw his lists of songs—longer than most of the inhabitants—whilst his other was thrust into his trowsers' pocket; the impudent leer upon his face, as he surveyed his audience, and the careless set of his clothes, which, big as he was, seemed a size too capacious for him,—immediately attracted a crowd. A butcher's dog, who had been ordered to make all speed to No. 10 in this same street with a leg of mutton in his basket, stayed to gape and listen, although he was standing opposite No. 9. A young pup from a neighbouring alley ran out at the sound of his voice to learn the news. A spaniel, with long curly hair and medicine-basket on his arm, could not resist the temptation of just stopping to hear, though three servants of one of his master's patients were scouring the streets in search of him; nor could an eminent vocalist of the feline tribe, la Signorina Pussetta Scracciolini, pass by without lending an ear to the wonderful list of melodies. There was another figure, too, who slackened her pace as she was passing the group, and by an irresistible impulse seemed compelled to draw near and listen; she was richly dressed in mantle and hood, which, thrown gracefully back, displayed a head and neck of aristocratic proportions; she seemed ill, however, and weak, for her delicate paws were resting on a stick, as though such aid were requisite, whilst her short breathing seemed to hint that her sorrows were bringing her nearer to her doom. She must have been once possessed of considerable beauty, and even now there was enough remaining to distinguish the Hon. Miss Greyhound.

Thus surrounded, Bruin vociferated with all the power of his lungs,—

"O ... O ... O ... O ... O ... Y .... A! Never were such times! Here you are! only look! Double your own length of songs for one penny! Enough paper to make yourselves a coat to wrap yourselves in melody! Only one penny! Five hundred of the choicest songs of the Caterwaullic and Puppeeyan Amalgamated Harmonic Societies; and upwards of five hundred more of the most popular ditties of Caneville, and all for one penny!!"

And then he croaked forth the following doggerel (the most acceptable poetry, by the way, of the city), in which the titles of the songs were dragged in, without any regard to order, to make up a rhyme:

"Here's 'What's a Clock?'
And 'Like a rock
He stood upon his dignity;'
With 'Pups alive,'
And 'We are Five,'
And dozens more. Who'll buy? who'll buy?
Here's 'Puss was out,'
And 'Piggy's snout
Was longer far than I can tell;'
With 'Merry Dogs,'
And 'Yellow Frogs'
In scores, I'm ready here to sell.
Here's 'Burning sighs,'
And, 'Ah! those eyes!'
And 'Songs for kittens newly born;'
With 'Stay, oh, stay!'
And 'Don't say nay,'
And some no worse for being worn.
Here's 'Love's an ass!'
And 'Pass the glass,'
And 'Jocky is the dog for me;'
Here's 'Did you ever?'
'No, I never!'
And 'I hope it yet may be,'
And all for one penny!"

And thus he went down the street disposing of his wares with wonderful rapidity, and producing sundry forced accompaniments to his own wretched song by treading on the toes of all the pups who were attracted by curiosity to his vicinity.

A second and a third supply was exhausted before the canine and feline public of Caneville got tired of purchasing their own measure of song; whether a fourth would have been successful there was no chance of discovering, for Old Powtry looked in vain for Bruin with the proceeds of the last lot. Day after day passed by and still he was absent, until it was deemed necessary to have a search after him. For some time he eluded all inquiries, as he well knew his fate if his hiding-place were discovered; for having appropriated the money of his master to his own use, he was fully aware that his person would have to pay the penalty of his transgression. He skulked about the lowest purlieus of the city, among curs of the most degraded character, as dirty and negligent in body as they were debased in mind, until, in hourly fear of being betrayed, he felt that the worst certainty would be preferable to such a state of suspense and alarm, so resolved to deliver himself up and brave the worst. He was again cast into prison: for that he was prepared; but he was *not* prepared for the wretched place of confinement to which he was now condemned. On being first thrust into it, he could not behold all its horror; but when his eyes got accustomed to the semi-darkness, he found himself in a dismal cell under ground, half full of water from the overflowing of the river, and teeming with numerous crawling, slimy things. A little hole, half choked with earth and stones, let in all the place possessed of light and air; and as the only air which could ever visit the place had to pass over a bed of stagnant mud ere it reached the spot, it possessed but few refreshing properties.

Bruin, who had in his despair given himself quietly up to the authorities, thinking probably that by the very act he might procure some mitigation of his sentence, now that he perceived his doom, gave way to one of those fearful bursts of rage which no experience had succeeded in teaching him to curb. He howled till the dirt sticking about the vaulted ceiling, and the earth choking up the air-hole, dropped piecemeal to the ground, and every insect that had ears covered them up the best way it could to prevent its becoming instantaneously deafened by the horrid sound; then tearing round and round and round the confined space of his cell, till there seemed to him fifty windows instead of one, and the single door appeared suddenly placed in every part of the miserable vault,—he struck his head against the rugged wall of his prison, and toppled over senseless on to the ground.

AT REST.

It is not easy to say how long Bruin remained insensible, but it must have been some time; for when he recovered himself, there was a feeling of weakness about him as though he had been fasting long. His head, too, felt sadly dizzy as he rose from his cold bed and pushed his nose against the hole of a window to procure a little air. From this he withdrew to pace his narrow cell; and as the turning round increased his giddiness, on reaching the opposite wall he retraced his steps backwards, and so continued for a full hour, gently moving his head meanwhile to the right and left, as was his wont. Then getting into the driest corner, he threw himself of a heap on the ground, and mechanically resuming the old family practice of sucking his paw, tried to bring his mind to bear upon his situation. But this was a matter of no little difficulty, for the late events of his life had tended very considerably to weaken an intellect that was never remarkable for strength; and so he sat, and relapsed into a dozy state, where forgetfulness, for the most part, presided. At times, it is true, he would wake up, and the old fire lighting in his eyes, he would dash his paw on the ground as he observed the prison-walls close around him; but the feeling was momentary, and it was evident that the indulgence of his evil passions had so far clouded his reason, that a few weeks' solitary confinement would deprive him of all power of reflection for ever.

Evening had come again, though it was dark night in Bruin's cell, and had been so for hours; when suddenly he heard, or fancied he heard, his name uttered in a loud whisper. A fear he had never before experienced, an apprehension of he knew not what, stole over him; and it was not till the voice, a little louder, exclaimed,—

"Bruin! Bruin, I say!" that he dared venture a reply; when, after an effort, he said,—

"Who calls?"

"A friend," was the ready answer.

"A friend!" exclaimed Bruin, savagely; "then you can't be seeking *me*, for I have got no friends."

"Come, come, Bruin," said the voice again, "don't be testy; it's I, the Captain, and you know I never played you false."

Bruin now, indeed, recognised the voice as that of, perhaps, the most desperate dog in Caneville. He was a bloodhound of large size and formidable strength, and such ferocity and daring, that few cared to come into contact with him, lest by some chance they should be involved in a quarrel which could only have a disastrous termination. Public report fixed more than one deep crime upon this canine desperado; but still, somehow, he escaped the power of the law. Bruin felt flattered at his attention, and inquired what had brought him there.

"Why," replied the Captain, "this is the third time I have been here already; but though I have called out your name so loudly that I expected to alarm the guard, I have got no answer till to-night. I shouldn't have come back again, for I thought you were dead."

"So I have been nearly, Captain," answered Bruin; "but I am not quite gone yet, you hear. Now you *have* found me alive, though, what is it you want; and how can I, shut up here, be of any interest to you?"

"Listen to me, Bruin," said the Captain, as he squeezed his nose into the tiny window, and dropped his voice to a low whisper; "if you were out, and at liberty, would you feel inclined to join me and one or two others in a job we intend to come off to-night?"

Bruin hastened to reply, but the Captain interrupted him, saying,—

"Don't be in a hurry to make a promise, until you know what it is; for, shut up here as you are, you can't betray the secret if you would, so I don't mind revealing it. Four of us mean to break into old Lord Greyhound's house to-night, where we hear there's money enough to enrich us for our lives; but as we're likely to have some hard work and stout resistance, and think we are not strong enough yet for the business, we should like you to join us, if you choose to do so."

Bruin reflected a moment, where reflection was ruin. Had he at once and scornfully rejected the horrible temptation, there would still have been hope for him; but, besides the prospect of liberty, though he did not yet know how that was to be effected, there was the chance of enriching himself once again; and, above all, there was a prospect of revenge against the dog who had once sought his life, because he had been selected as an object of preference by his daughter. His meditations, therefore, were at once brought to an end, by his resolution to accept the proposal; but before he did so, the caution he had acquired by associating with such beasts as the Captain made him say,—

"Let us understand each other clearly. You said just now, 'if I were out and at liberty;' have you, then, the power to set me free?"

"Provided you will be of the party, and agree to our terms," answered the Captain.

"And how if I refuse?" pursued Bruin.

"Why," replied the Captain, quickly and ferociously, "you'll stop there till you starve."

"I accept your offer," said Bruin, after the slightest possible pause; "and I would have done so without the alternative, for private reasons of my own: so let me out, old fellow, as fast as you like."

"And you give your word?" said the Captain.

"The word of a bear," replied Bruin.

The other exclaimed,—

"All right! I shall see you again in half an hour."

Never did half hour seem so long. As minute after minute flew by, there broke upon Bruin's misty brain a notion that, perhaps, this was only a trick of the Captain's to get him to declare his willingness to join any desperate deed in order to ruin him; but then, again, he could discover no reason for such enmity, and could see no advantage accruing to that individual by such a course. At the very idea, however, of such betrayal, his teeth gnashed together, his eyes glared in that darkness like two live coals, and he involuntarily crossed his huge paws over his chest as though hugging some imaginary enemy. But he recovered his self-possession on hearing a grating noise at the other side of the cell, which gradually became louder, until at last a gust of air, which revived his spirits, came whistling round the vault, and told that his path was open. The Captain, too, was in an instant by his side to confirm it. He passed through an aperture, caused by an open iron door, preceded by his companion, who had, however, first cautiously reclosed and fastened up the secret entrance; and as they traversed a damp and dark tunnel, the Captain explained the mystery, by saying this place had been known to him some time, though it was unsuspected by the authorities; and that the exterior entrance was so covered up by brambles, that no one ignorant of the spot could ever imagine what lay behind, or would care to explore the threatening passage, if by any chance they discovered it.

As Bruin was exhausted for want of food, and it still wanted some hours of the time appointed for their undertaking, they proceeded to one of the old resorts and regaled most heartily, the sense of liberty after his confinement raising the bear's spirits to the highest pitch. At length the time agreed on arrived, and the party, prepared for their desperate and wicked undertaking, set out.

It has been mentioned in a previous part of this history, that Lord Greyhound was one of the principal grandees in Caneville, both as regarded fortune and family, and that he lived in a palace befitting his condition. A crowd of domestics belonged to his household, but the Captain was aware that their cribs were remote, and that but little in the shape of resistance was to be feared from them, should they be aroused. Still great caution was requisite, for if they did not bite they could bark, and that would be equally as fatal to their success on this occasion. The only difficulty to be got over was the vigilance of a porter who slept below, whose fidelity to his master had been tried on more than one occasion, although what made such attachment singular in this instance was the fact that the said porter was one of the feline tribe,—a cat, in fact, of large dimensions, and peculiarly savage nature. Bruin, however, took upon himself the task of quieting this servant and keeping watch below, whilst the others should ransack the mansion, a place of rendezvous being appointed where they were to meet in case of alarm.

To avoid suspicion they proceeded alone to the scene of their intended crime, and, favoured by darkness, they reached it unchallenged. Having gently tried the fastenings in one or two places, they resolved to make the attempt at a small door at the back, which seemed the most weakly guarded. Bruin pushed it first quietly with his huge shoulder, and finding it gradually yielding, without farther ado he placed his knee against the lower panel, and, with less noise than might have been expected, sent the door flying from its fastenings. He was the first to enter, though the others were close behind; but he had not taken two steps within the house than he saw, as he thought, two balls of fire on the floor before him,—it was his last look of worldly things,—for at the same moment the porter Cat, for it was he, sprang at the huge giant like a fury, and dug his long and pointed talons into Bruin's eyes. With a howl so dreadful, so awful in its intense agony and rage, that it seemed to spring from a supernatural source, the affrighted beast rolled over and over in his pain, crushing the Cat to death in his struggles; then feeling, even amidst his suffering, the necessity of safety, he rose to his feet, and ran on, on, on, he knew not whither, till he felt himself in the midst of water and heard the rushing which it made. So instantaneous had been the whole transaction that the truth was never rightly known. The family—nay, the neighbourhood—aroused by the horrid noise, rushed to the spot, to find the faithful porter dead, with every bone shattered; the door was open, but no creature was there to tell the tale. One alone suspected it—one to whom that cry of agony was the death-blow; for, two days after the event, the Hon. Miss Greyhound slept with her fathers, the victim of a misplaced and unworthy attachment.

And Bruin, where was he? Alas! poor beast! Three days after this event he was discovered by the authorities, half dead with pain, and led back to prison, which he had left with so little ceremony. His senses, however, were so bewildered by his situation, that he could neither explain how he had escaped from his dungeon, nor the cause of his present deplorable condition; perhaps, too, he deemed it more prudent to be silent on both these matters. His judges, nevertheless, taking into consideration his now helpless state, and rightly thinking his powers of mischief were much abated by the loss of his eyes, pardoned his previous offence, and thrust him alone and helpless on the world.

For many a long year did the ill-fated animal drag on his wearisome existence, living on the charity—the scanty charity—of Caneville. Deprived of sight, no longer able to acquire a livelihood by his labour, weary, and full of remorse, he daily took his round through the public streets, soliciting a penny for the "poor blind." A dog, induced for a weekly trifle and the prospect of an extra bone or two thrown to him, sometimes by the compassionate as they went their melancholy way, led him in his wanderings. At first, however, either from ignorance or carelessness, or a currish malice, he would often guide his helpless master into positions of difficulty and danger, from which he could scarce have extricated himself but for the assistance of some benevolent passers-by; though his situation in such cases—be it said to the shame of the inferior population of Caneville—too often excited derision and laughter, instead of aid and consolation. Once, indeed, he was seriously hurt by the wilful inattention of his guide; for, tottering along as usual, one fine morning with his staff in one hand, the string attached to the dog's collar in the other, and his head with the sightless eyes raised sadly in the air, whilst he uttered his plaintive cry of "Have pity on the poor blind!" the last word was suddenly converted from a doleful whine to a howl of pain as his body came in contact with a post which stood right across his path. Time, which cures all things, brought at last an effectual remedy to his sufferings, and that remedy was Death! Ere that great foe or friend relieved poor Bruin, he had learnt to be repentant of his former life, and was often known to reprove in others any tendency to those faults of temper or disposition which had been his own ruin. If he could have recovered the use of his eyes and have mingled once more with the business of life, it is a question whether he would have acted up to the precepts which he now inculcated; but as the experiment was never tried, nor could be, it is but charitable to think the best.

THE LAST LEAD.

Months after he had departed this sinful world, a sturdy traveller, with a particularly wide mouth and short address, entered the city of Caneville. He stated that he was a native of the place, and had been wandering far away in other lands. He made various inquiries concerning former inhabitants of the town, and among others asked for Bruin. His life, much as I have recounted it, was told to him, and long did the stranger ruminate over the details. Many portions of it were, indeed, known to him, for the traveller was no other than our old acquaintance Tom; but all was interesting. When he had heard it to the end, he uttered these only words, which might, indeed, serve for moral and poor Bruin's epitaph:—

"Ah! he was a Great Bear!"